My Vancouver Sketchbook

Robert Perry • Illustrations by Greta Guzek

NIGHTWOOD EDITIONS

"I am my sketchbook."

–Pablo Picasso,
Spanish artist

To sketch Vancouver
From dawn until dark,
From Spanish Banks
To Stanley Park,

I'll need my yellow,
Red, blue and green,
And all the colours
In between.

Sunrise Over Spanish Banks

Around Point Grey
A cedar canoe,
With paddles gleaming,
Glides into view.

And just out there,
On glittering waves,
Captain Vancouver
Meets Spanish gaze.

Nitobe Memorial Garden

HAIKU

The trees of Japan
Blossom in the rainforest—
A mirror garden!

Kitsilano

From Kitsilano,
Blue on blue,
The North Shore mountains
Recede from view.

All summer long
They set the stage
For song and dance
For every age.

Maritime Museum

The St. Roch braved
The Arctic ice
Of the Northwest Passage—
Not once—but twice!

We walk the deck,
Explore the hold—
Imagine the winds!
Imagine the cold!

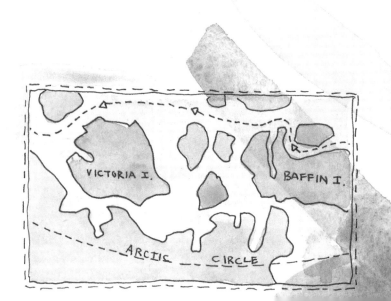

VICTORIA I.

BAFFIN I.

ARCTIC CIRCLE

Children's Festival

The giant tents
Are setting sail
With song and dance
And fairy tale;

With puppetry
And crafts and rhyme;
With acrobatics,
Juggling and mime.

To
Granville
Island!

Look through the bridge—
The island's the same
As a picture
Placed in a frame.

The ferryboats
Dart to and fro—
Under the bridge
Here we go!

Island of Artists

I feed the pigeons
Crumbs of bread,
Then watch them orbit
Above my head.

I've time to take
A short art lesson:
Painting the boats
Making an impression.

Woodcarver, woodcarver,
Carve me a boat
Of yellow cedar
That I can float!

English Bay

We race down the grass
To English Bay
To see the sails
Fly through the spray.

We count the freighters,
Anchored for days,
Rusting red
In the summer haze.

We unwind the string,
Spread out the tail—
Our homemade kite
Is under sail!

A perfect subject
For a still life painting:
A great blue heron
Patiently waiting.

Stanley Park Seawall

Round and round
From dawn until dark,
Everyone loves
To circle the park.

Stanley Park Aquarium

Way down deep
In the emerald sea
Someone's keeping
An eye on me.

Into the water,
Out of a glade,
The Canada geese
Love to parade.

What do I look like
When I pass
On the other side
Of the glass?

Robson Street

I love to dance
To the urban beat
Echoing down
Robson Street.

Vancouver
Art Gallery

People come
From near and far
To see the art
Of Emily Carr.

When she was just
A girl like me,
She painted the forest
By the sea.

Science World

Dream of sailing
Starlit seas
To other worlds
And galaxies.

Explore the world
That we call home
Inside the giant
Spangled dome.

Chinatown

Dragon red,
Peacock blue—
I've got to find
The perfect hue—

Neon yellow,
Garden green,
Black and white
And tangerine.

Commercial Drive

The city spills
Onto the street:
Try a latte
Or gelato treat!

Hear accents from
A hundred nations;
Enjoy the show
Of street-smart fashions.

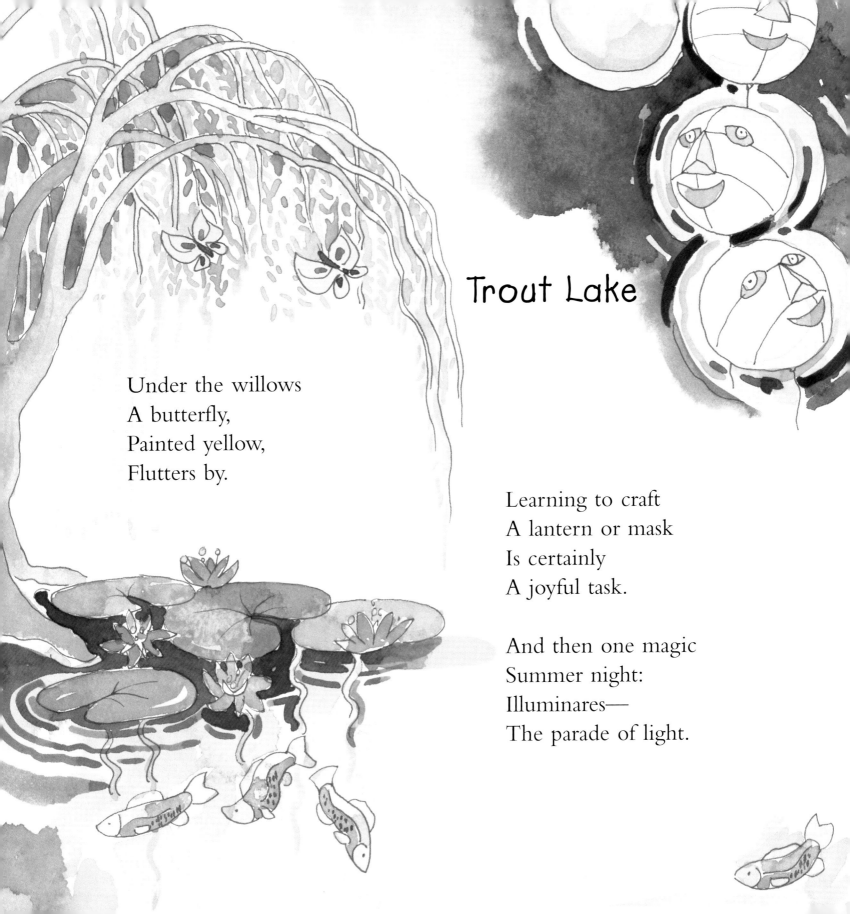

Trout Lake

Under the willows
A butterfly,
Painted yellow,
Flutters by.

Learning to craft
A lantern or mask
Is certainly
A joyful task.

And then one magic
Summer night:
Illuminares—
The parade of light.

Gastown

Look down the streets,
Hear shunting trains,
See cargo ships
And giant cranes,

Find the statue
Of "Gassy Jack,"
Watch the steam clock
Blow its stack.

Seabus Ride!

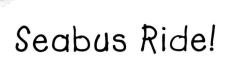

Come to the window!
Hold on to the rail!
One of us
Is under sail!

There's a ship
Loaded with freight!
There's Sulphur Mountain!
There's Lions Gate!

Lighthouse Park

Tonight, tonight,
A joyful sight:
The lighthouse will
Be spreading light.

Towboats and barges,
Sailboats, freighters,
Kayaks, cruisers,
Trawlers, seiners.

The centuries come,
The centuries go,
Ring on ring
The fir trees grow.

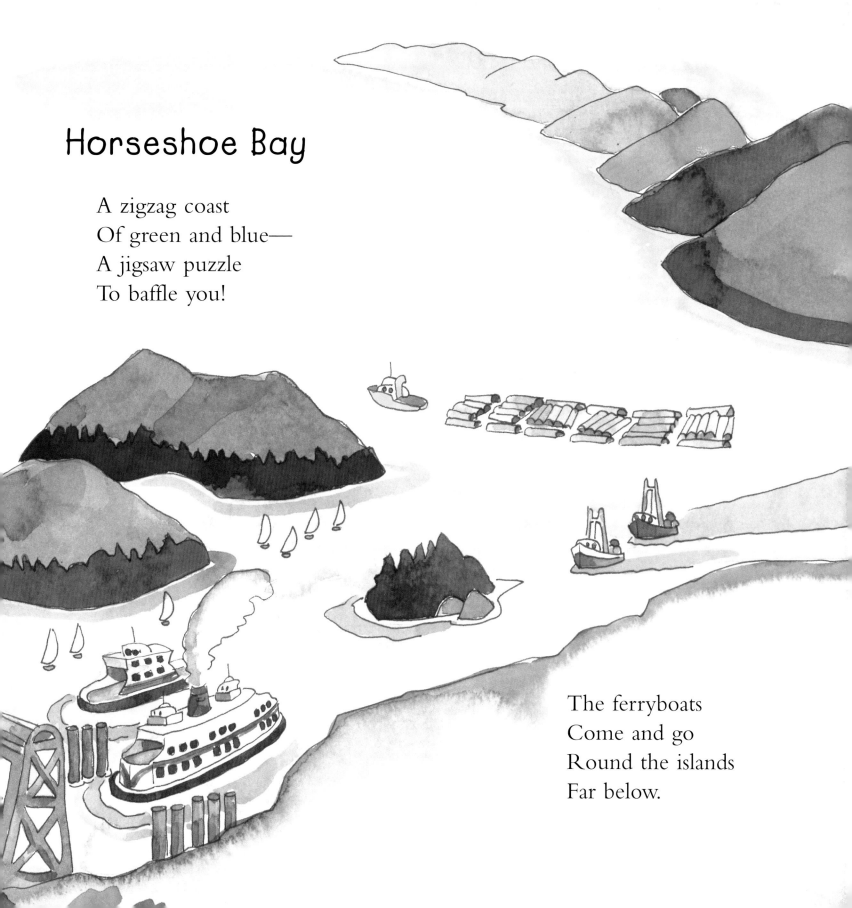

Horseshoe Bay

A zigzag coast
Of green and blue—
A jigsaw puzzle
To baffle you!

The ferryboats
Come and go
Round the islands
Far below.

Capilano Suspension Bridge

Above the river,
Among the trees,
The narrow bridge
Swings in the breeze.

I watch an eagle
In wheeling flight—
I'm getting dizzy!
Hold on tight!

Grouse Mountain

Vancouver lights
Sparkle and play—
We're sailing through
The Milky Way!

A happy day
Has flown away—
But in my book
I've made it stay.

Bye!

Marina

Text Copyright © 2001 by Robert Perry
Artwork Copyright © 2001 by Greta Guzek

First paperback edition published in 2010 by Nightwood Editions
1 2 3 4 5 — 14 13 12 11 10

Nightwood Editions
P.O. Box 1779
Gibsons, BC, V0N 1V0
Canada
www.nightwoodeditions.com

Canada Council   Conseil des Arts
for the Arts   du Canada

BRITISH
COLUMBIA
ARTS COUNCIL

Edited by Simone Doust
Jacket and interior design by Val Speidel
Manufactured by Prolong Press Ltd, China, January 2010, Job #1235/2498

Nightwood Editions acknowledges financial support from the Government of
Canada through the Book Publishing Industry Development Program and the
Canada Council for the Arts, and from the Province of British Columbia
through the BC Arts Council and the Book Publishing Tax Credit.

LIBRARY AND ARCHIVES CANADA CATALOGUING IN PUBLICATION

Perry, Robert Graham, 1951-
        My Vancouver sketchbook / Robert Perry ; illustrations
by Greta Guzek.

Reading grade level: K and up.
Interest age level: 5-10.
ISBN 978-0-88971-248-5

        1. Vancouver (B.C.)—Juvenile poetry.
I. Guzek, Greta II. Title.

FC3847.33.P47 2009   jC811'.54   C2009-907419-2